Fairies of
Blossom Bakery

Cookie

and the

Secret Sleepover

Picture Corgi

For Romy and Merryn, with love – M.A.
To Millie, Abbie and Autumn with love – K.H-J.

FAIRIES OF BLOSSOM BAKERY: COOKIE AND THE SECRET SLEEPOVER
A PICTURE CORGI BOOK 978 0 552 56901 9 Published in Great Britain by Picture Corgi, an imprint of Random House Children's Publishers UK A Random House Group Company This edition published 2013

1 3 5 7 9 10 8 6 4 2

Copyright © Random House Children's Publishers UK, 2013 Written by Mandy Archer Illustrated by Kirsteen Harris-Jones The right of Mandy Archer and Kirsteen Harris-Jones to be identified as the author and illustrator of this work has been asserted in accordance with the Copyright, Designs and Patents Act 1988. All rights reserved. Picture Corgi Books are published by Random House Children's Publishers UK, 61–63 Uxbridge Road, London W5 5SA

www.randomhousechildrens.co.uk
www.randomhouse.co.uk

Addresses for companies within The Random House Group Limited can be found at: www.randomhouse.co.uk/offices.htm THE RANDOM HOUSE GROUP Limited Reg. No. 954009 A CIP catalogue record for this book is available from the British Library. Printed in Italy

Plum

Cookie

Fairies of Blossom Bakery

Over the hills in a land of sweetness,
little fairies bake and play.
Would you like to peep at their secret,
scrumptious world?

Make a wish, then step
into the magic of Fairycake Kingdom
and meet the fairies…

Cupcake

Butterfly

Sparkle

Button

Pitter-patter-pitter-patter-pat!
Shimmering raindrops were falling outside, but Cookie the fairy didn't mind a bit. She was having a baking afternoon at Cupcake's house! Cupcake lived above the Blossom Bakery and Café – the most scrumptious eaterie in Fairycake Kingdom.

"I'll fetch the recipe books," said Cookie, fluttering up to the bookshelf.

"Isn't this fun?" giggled Cupcake. "We can bake something nice for our fairy friends."

Cookie smiled. Button, Butterfly, Plum and Sparkle all loved sweet treats!

Cookie and Cupcake were trying out new shortbread recipes.
The friends crumbled in chocolate chips and raisins, marshmallow
and fudge. Each warm, doughy delight tasted yummier than the last!

The rainy afternoon passed in a trice.

"Look at the time!" gasped Cupcake. "It will be getting dark soon."

"I'd better flutter home," said Cookie, untying her apron.

Cupcake wrapped up a parcel of shortbread for Cookie to share with the other fairies.

"Goodnight, Cupcake," said Cookie, waving. "See you tomorrow!"

"What a shame you have to go," Cupcake sighed dreamily. "Thank you for a lovely afternoon."

"It really is a shame," thought Cookie, tiptoeing up her garden path.
"I wish our baking dates lasted longer."

Suddenly Cookie had a magical idea! She hurried inside and got to work.

Bright and early the next morning, an envelope slipped through the Blossom Bakery letterbox.

"It's an invitation," gasped Cupcake. "From Cookie!"

Dearest Cupcake,
You are invited to a special secret sleepover
on Saturday night
at my house.

We can do baking, tell fairy stories and
share a magical midnight feast!

Please come at 6 o'clock.

Lots of love,
Your best fairy friend
Cookie xxx

When Cookie arrived at the Fairy Academy, all her friends were
waiting for her.

"Morning!" cried Button. "How was your baking date?"

Sparkle's face lit up. "Did you have fun at Cupcake's house?"

"I do hope so," added Plum kindly.

"I bet it was scrummy!" said Butterfly.

"It was delightful," Cookie told them, "thank you."

The fairies skipped into spell-casting class.

"Let's begin," called Madame Drizzle. "Hold out your wands please!"

Cookie tried to listen, but she couldn't stop dreaming about the secret sleepover invitation. It was going to be wonderful!

At lunchtime, Cookie gave out the shortbread she'd baked with Cupcake.

"Thank you," said Butterfly. "Let's meet up and eat it together!"

"Oh, yes!" exclaimed Button. "Come to my house on Saturday. We can work on our wishing-spell homework."

Sparkle beamed. "Are you free, Cookie?"

Cookie didn't know what to do! Suddenly she was nodding, but inside her heart skipped a beat.

"Let's meet at five o'clock," suggested Plum.

Cookie so wanted to tell her friends that she'd invited Cupcake for a sleepover instead, but it was a special secret. She decided not to say anything.

That way she wasn't fibbing, was she?

After class, the friends stopped in at the Blossom Bakery.
The café was very busy. Gnomes, elves and fairies sat
chattering at every table.

"Hello, Cupcake," said Plum. "Need any help?"

"Yes please!" replied Cupcake, carrying a tray of teacups.

While her other friends served the customers, Cookie went inside to do the dishes.

"Thank you for the invitation," said Cupcake. "The answer's 'yes please'. We're all going to have a super time!"

"Not 'all'," whispered Cookie. "Just you and me. It's a secret sleepover."

Cupcake blinked in surprise. "Oh."

On Saturday, Cookie popped a golden coin in her purse and set out for the Elf Market. She had a long list of things to buy.

Hot Chocolate
Marshmallows
Blankets
Slippers
Music
Delicious Recipe

First she bought some delicious hot chocolate and marshmallows.

Then she filled her basket with soft gossamer blankets . . .

. . . silkworm slippers,

enchanting music to
soothe them to sleep,

and a recipe for two beautiful
best friends' biscuits.
   Everything had to be perfect
for the secret sleepover!

After the market Cookie rushed to the General Store, a cascade of fairy dust shimmering behind her.

"Hello, Nana Puff," she cried. "Can I buy some butter, eggs and sugar?"

Nana Puff pointed to an empty glass jar on the counter. "Sorry, sweetness," she said. "Sugar's sold out! Button bought the last of it this morning."

Cookie didn't know what to do. She couldn't make best friends'
biscuits without any sugar!

"I can't ask Cupcake to lend me some," she sighed. "It will spoil
the surprise."

The little fairy wriggled her nose – could she ask the other fairies
without giving away her secret?

Button and the other fairies were just finishing tea when Cookie tapped on the door.

"There you are!" snapped Sparkle. "We saved you a piece of shortbread."

Cookie's wings drooped forlornly. "I–I can't stay," she mumbled quietly, "but I wondered if I could borrow some sugar?"

The fairies gathered around her looking a bit cross.

"Why do you need sugar?" Button asked. "We thought you were coming over to work on Madame Drizzle's homework?"

Little tears fell like raindrops down Cookie's cheeks.

"Cupcake and I had so much fun last weekend, I invited her for a sleepover at my house," she sobbed. "I should have said something when you asked me to come here instead, but I didn't want to let any of you down. I'm so sorry!"

"You can always be honest with us," smiled Button. "You should have said that you wanted to do something with Cupcake. We could have met up another day."

"I wanted it to be a best-friends thing," whispered Cookie. "What a silly secret."

"But we are all your friends, and true friends will always understand," cried Button, Sparkle, Plum and Butterfly.

Cookie gasped. She was being wrapped in the tightest fairy hug ever!

Cookie was SO happy: she knew she'd been silly, but she also knew she had the best friends in the world.

She looked up at the clock. Cupcake would be coming over soon!

"Will you come and join us at the sleepover?" she asked earnestly. "All of you?"

Butterfly did a fairy cartwheel. Sparkle and Plum clapped their hands.

"I'll get the sugar," giggled Button.

When Cupcake fluttered round to Cookie's house, a magical surprise was waiting for her.

"Five fairy friends!" she gasped. "What a treat!"

"That's right," agreed Cookie. "It's my special sleepover secret!"

The fairies chattered, swapped cuddly toys and showed off their pyjamas. Everybody agreed that it was going to be the best sleepover ever!

"What shall we bake tonight?" asked Button.

Cookie thought for a moment. She only had enough ingredients for two best friends' biscuits. Then the clever little fairy spotted her cookie cutter set. "Let's make lots of mini biscuits," she suggested. "They're just right for sharing!"

There was a flurry of excited giggles as everyone got to work.

"What special friends," whispered Cookie. "I'm such a lucky fairy!"

Mini chocolate-dipped hearts

Small heart-cut cookies with their tops dipped in dark chocolate

Shopping list for at least 24 heart cookies

- 75g unsalted butter
- 75g light brown sugar
- 3 tablespoons golden syrup
- 200g plain flour, plus extra for sprinkling
- 1 teaspoon baking powder
- 1 teaspoon ground ginger
- 1 teaspoon cinnamon
- 100g bar dark chocolate
- Small heart-shaped cookie cutter
- Rolling pin

Always ask a grown-up to help you in the kitchen, especially when using the oven.

To make the cookies:

1. Ask a grown-up to pre-heat the oven to 180°C/350°F/Gas Mark 4. Line a baking tray with a sheet of greaseproof paper.

2. Put the butter, sugar and golden syrup into a non-stick saucepan. Ask your grown-up to put the pan on a very low heat. Use a wooden spoon to gently stir the ingredients until everything has melted.

3. Tip the flour, baking powder, ginger and cinnamon into a clean bowl, then scrape in the sticky mixture from the saucepan. Stir everything together. Before long, your mixture will have formed a delicious-smelling dough. Sprinkle some flour on your worktop and place the dough on top.

4. Use a rolling pin to roll the dough out. If it gets stuck to the worktop, just sprinkle on a little more flour. When the dough is flat and about as thick as the wooden spoon handle you're ready to cut out your heart cookies. Carefully press out little hearts using your special cookie cutter and place them on the baking tray. When you've finished, ask your grown-up to pop the tray in the oven.

5. Bake the cookies for around 10 minutes. When they are ready, each one will turn a light golden brown. That's the time your grown-up should take the cookies out and put them on a wire rack to cool.

6. Ask your grown-up to melt the chocolate in a bowl over a pan of hot water, while you lay another sheet of greaseproof paper on to a serving plate. When the chocolate is safely off the heat, carefully dip the top of each heart into the bowl, then lay it on the paper.

7. Pop your chocolaty heart cookies into the fridge to set. After an hour, take the cookies out and serve them all to your fairy friends!

Fairy Tip
Fairies always wash their hands before starting a new recipe!

Bye-bye for now!

We hope you enjoyed your visit
to the Fairycake Kingdom.

Please join us again for more adventures!